# panda series

**PANDA books are for first readers beginning to make their own way through books.**

D1630889

# Helpful
# Hannah

Written and illustrated by
• MARIE BURLINGTON •

THE O'BRIEN PRESS
DUBLIN

First published 2004 by The O'Brien Press Ltd,
12 Terenure Road East, Rathgar, Dublin 6, Ireland.
Tel: +353 1 4923333; Fax: +353 1 4922777
E-mail: books@obrien.ie
Website: www.obrien.ie
Reprinted 2005, 2007.

ISBN: 978-0-86278-837-7

British Library Cataloguing-in-Publication Data
A catalogue reference for this title is available from the British Library

3   4   5   6   7   8   9   10
07  08  09  10  11  12  13

The O'Brien Press receives
assistance from

the arts
council
schomhairle
ealaíon

Typesetting, layout, editing, design: The O'Brien Press Ltd
Printing: Cox & Wyman Ltd

Can YOU spot the panda
hidden in the story?

Hannah lived with her granny.
They lived in an
old, old house
at the end of a
long, long lane.

6

Hannah was very good
at fixing things.

This was very useful
because Granny's old house
was full of **creaks**
and **cracks**
and **moans**
and **groans**.

9

Hannah had her own toolbox
with **oil**
and **screwdrivers**
and **nuts**
and **bolts**
and **nails** ...
and lots of other useful things.

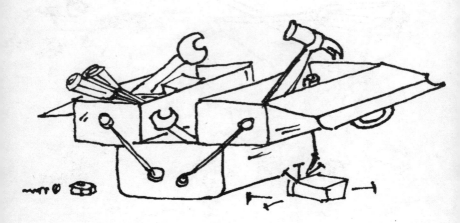

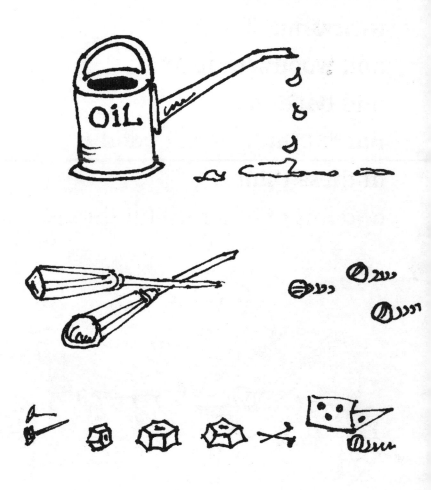

Hannah's granny liked
to arrange flowers,
knit woolly jumpers
and bake cakes.
But Hannah wasn't good
at these things.

'Can you put these flowers
in that vase, Hannah?'
said Granny.

Hannah tried, but
**snap**, **snap**, **snap**,
the stems dropped off, and
**flop**, **flop**, **flop**,
the flowers bent over.
It was a mess!

'Oh dear,' said Granny.

**'I tried my best**,'
said Hannah.

Hannah tried to knit.
**Click**, **click**, **click**
went the needles,
but the wool got tangled up
and her knitting was
**full of holes**.

'Oh dear,' said Granny.

**'I tried my best**,'
said Hannah.

Hannah tried to bake bread.
**Stir**, **stir**, **stir**, she went,
but the bread was so hard
even the birds
turned up their beaks at it!

'Oh dear,' said Granny.

**'I tried my best**,'
said Hannah.

But Hannah loved to learn
how to fix things.
When she walked down
the long, long lane,
she often saw Old Joe Coady
mending things.

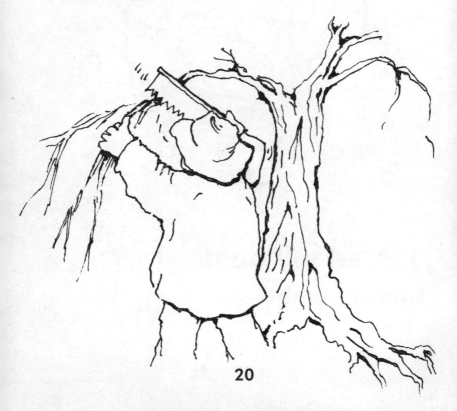

One day he was
trying to fix his gate.

**Squeak, squeak, squeak,**
it went.

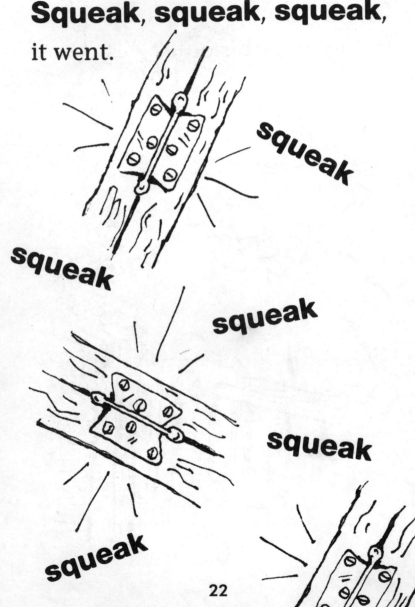

squeak

squeak

squeak

squeak

squeak

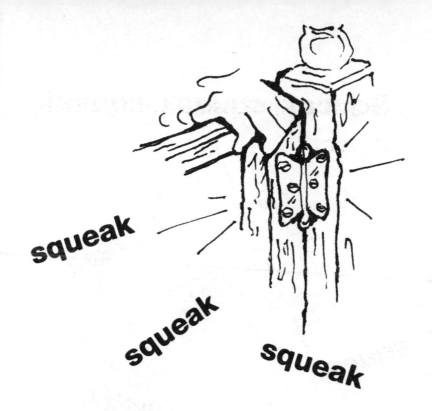

**squeak**

**squeak**

**squeak**

Every time he moved the gate
it squeaked.

'Oh no,' said Joe. 'I'm out of oil.'

'But **I'm** not,' said Hannah.

She dripped the oil
on to the rusty hinge.

'As good as new,' said Joe.
'Thank you, Hannah.'

Further down the lane
she saw Mrs White
fixing a plant on her wall.
But it kept slipping off the nail.

'Will you hold this
for me, Hannah?'
said Mrs White.

'I'll do better than that,'
said Hannah.
'I've got some stronger nails.
I'll fix it up for you.'

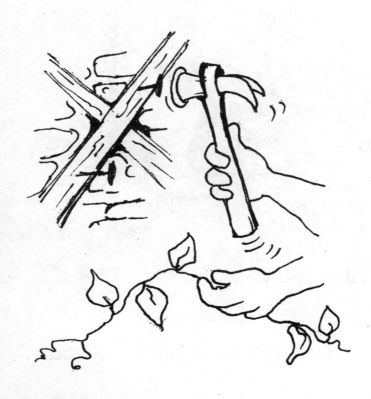

**Tap, tap, tap** ...

Hannah hammered in the nails.

Then they hung up the plant.

'As good as new!'

said Mrs White.

'Thank you so much, Hannah.'

Sam White was
mending a puncture.
'Hey! Hannah!' he called.
'Help!'

'Here, hold this
while I get some water,' he said.
Hannah did.

Then she held the spanner
while Sam tested the tube
to see where the puncture was.
He covered the hole
with a patch.

'Brill!' he said. 'Hannah,
you're a star!'

But Granny didn't think
Hannah was a star!
Granny bought Hannah
a dolls' house.

'Just right for a **little girl**,'
said Granny.

'Fantastic!' said Hannah.
'Just the thing for my
**ant collection**.'

Granny sighed.

Granny gave Hannah
her old handbag.

'You might like to keep
your little treasures
in that, dear,'
said Granny.

Hannah had a great idea!

It was just perfect for
**her spiders**.

When Granny opened the bag
she screamed so loudly
the birds flew away
and didn't come home
for a week.

Granny gave up.
'You can use the garden shed
for your tools, Hannah,'
she said.

'Wow, my very own workshop,'
said Hannah. 'Brill!
Thanks, Gran.'

Granny helped Hannah
clean out the garden shed.
Out went a rickety old rake.

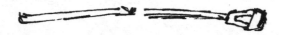

Out went an old broken hoe.

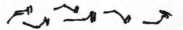

Out went some rusty nails.

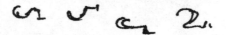

Out went bent old hooks.
Out went a shabby suitcase.

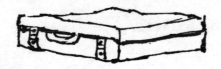

Out went a twisted old
tennis racket.
'I used to play tennis with that
when I was a girl,' said Granny.
She looked sad.

Quietly Hannah took it back
and put it in a corner.

Hannah looked at
**her new workshop**.
'Cool,' she said.
'Thanks, Gran. I love it.'

She had kept some old shelves
and an old pram.
And the tennis racket,
of course.

Hannah had her plans!

All day long
Hannah worked
in her workshop.
**Crash**, **bang**, **wallop**,
was all Granny heard.

'Oh dear,' Granny sighed.
'Oh dear, oh dear.
My little girl has
turned into a carpenter ...
and a mechanic ...
and a builder!'

One morning Hannah
looked out her window.
A thick blanket of snow
covered the ground.
The wind blew and
the storm howled.

'I'm not feeling well,'
said Granny.
Hannah phoned the doctor.
'I can't drive up with
the ice and snow, Hannah,'
said Dr Murphy.
'Try and get your Gran
down to Mrs White's house.'

Hannah raced to her workshop.
Out came a sleigh
she had made out of
the broken shelves and pram.

'I can push you down the lane,'
said Hannah.

'Amazing!' said Granny,
and she settled herself
on the sleigh.

'**Wheeeee**!' cried Granny
as they flew down the lane.
She felt better already.
Soon she was fine again.

But Hannah had plans
for Granny.

Granny was old and she found
a lot of things hard to do.
Hannah decided to
make things easier for Granny.

'Can you reach up, love,
and get me the duster,'
Granny said next day.

'You can do that yourself,'
said Hannah. 'Here!'
She had fixed a hook
on to a broom handle for Gran.
'Great!' said Granny.

Granny went to pick up
leaves in the garden.
'Oh my back!' she said.
'Can you pick them up,
Hannah?'

'Here,' said Hannah.
She had fixed a fork on to
an old rake handle.
'Excellent!' said Granny.

'I'm going to bake
an apple tart,' said Granny.
'Hannah, can you go and
get some apples off the tree?'

Out came a long handle
with a bent hook on the end.

'You can pull them down
with this,' said Hannah.
'Wonderful!' said Granny.

Granny looked under the stairs.
She had kept one large suitcase.
'**I** need a tool box **now**,'
said Granny.
And what useful tools
they all were.

'Well done, Hannah,'
said Granny. 'You're great!'

**'I tried my best,'**
said Hannah.
They both laughed.

Hannah had
**one more surprise**
for Granny.

Hannah worked and worked
in her workshop.
Whenever Granny
came to chat,
Hannah hid her work.

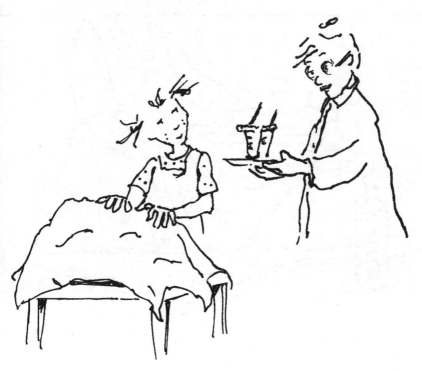

Soon it was Granny's birthday.
'Happy birthday, Granny,'
said Hannah.

She gave Granny
a big parcel.
It was wrapped in
beautiful coloured paper.

'Now, what could **this** be?'
said Granny.
'Something **very useful**,
I'm sure.
Something new
for my tool box!'

'Three guesses,' said Hannah.

Granny felt the parcel.
'A special hook for
getting down my saucepans?'
'No,' said Hannah.

'A tool for turning off the taps
in my bath?'
'Wrong,' said Hannah.
'One more guess.'

'Hmm!' said Granny.
'It's a ... It's a ....
I haven't a clue, Hannah.
What **IS** it?'

Hannah smiled.

'Open it, Granny!' she said.

And Granny opened it.

It wasn't a stick for getting
down saucepans.

It wasn't a tool for
turning off taps.

It wasn't even **useful**.

It was a **special picture**
for Granny.

Granny smiled.
'This takes me back …' she said.
'You **are** a sweet girl, Hannah.'